Henry and Mudge
AND THE
Happy Cat

The Eighth Book of Their Adventures

Story by Cynthia Rylant
Pictures by Suçie Stevenson

Aladdin Paperbacks

To the Peacocks: Nancy,
Larry, Aaron, and Natalie—CR

For Chuck, Kathy, and Jack—SS

Aladdin Paperbacks
An imprint of Simon & Schuster
Children's Publishing Division
1230 Avenue of the Americas
New York, NY 10020
Text copyright © 1990 by Cynthia Rylant
Illustrations copyright © 1990 by Suçie Stevenson
First Aladdin Paperbacks edition, 1994

Printed in the United States of America

10 9 8 7 6 5 4

The text of this book is set in 18 point Goudy Old Style.
The illustrations are pen-and-ink and watercolor, reproduced in full color.
Series designed by Mina Greenstein.
A hardcover edition of Henry and Mudge and Happy Cat is available from
Bradbury Press, an affiliate of Macmillan, Inc.

Library of Congress Cataloging-in-Publication Data
Rylant, Cynthia.
    Henry and Mudge and the happy cat : the eighth book of their
adventures / story by Cynthia Rylant ; pictures by Suçie Stevenson.—
1st Aladdin Books ed.
        p.   cm.
    Summary: Henry's family takes in a stray cat, the ugliest cat they have
ever seen, and an amazing relationship blossoms between it and their big
dog Mudge.
    ISBN 0-689-71791-1
    [1. Cats—Fiction. 2. Dogs—fiction.]   I. Stevenson, Suçie, ill.
II. Title.
[PZ7.R982Hi   1994]
[E]—dc20   93-10797

Contents

What Is It?

One night Henry
and Henry's father
and Henry's big dog Mudge
were watching TV.

5

Suddenly Mudge ran
to the door
and barked.

Henry's father opened
the door. Sitting
on the steps was
the shabbiest cat
Henry had ever seen.

It had a saggy belly,
skinny legs,
and fur that looked like
mashed prunes.
Henry and Henry's father
and Henry's big dog Mudge
stood in the door
and looked at the shabby cat.
"Hey kitty," said Henry.
"Are you sure it's a kitty?"
said Henry's father.

"It might be a stray,"
Henry said, petting it.
"It has to be," said Henry's father.
"That is the shabbiest cat
I have ever seen."

He carried the cat
into the house while
Henry and Mudge followed.
Mudge's tail was wagging hard.

"This cat looks like
mashed prunes," said Henry.
"But it's nice."
"Nice for a disaster,"
said Henry's father.

The three of them watched
as the cat drank three
bowls of milk in a row.

"Can it stay?" Henry asked.
"Only until we find a home
for it," said his father.
He looked hard at the cat.

"Do you think it *knows*
it's that shabby?" Henry's father asked.

Mudge was licking some milk

from the visitor's chin.

"Mudge doesn't know,"

Henry said.

"Mudge likes it."

"Yes," said Henry's father,

"but Mudge also likes turkey gizzards."

A Good Mother

In one week the shabby cat
turned into a happy cat.
It loved three things
about Henry's house.
It loved the towel closet.
It loved the bathtub.

And it loved Mudge.

In one week
the shabby cat had become
Mudge's mother.

It washed Mudge all the time.
It washed Mudge's ears.
It washed Mudge's eyes.
It even washed Mudge's dirty feet.
"*Yuck*," said Henry.

The cat also made Mudge
use good manners.
Mudge had to wait his turn
at the water dish.

Mudge had to share
his dog toys.

Mudge even had to share his crackers.
But Mudge didn't mind,
because Mudge loved the cat, too.

Henry's mother and Henry's father
wondered what they would do
with the cat.
They liked it.
But taking care of Mudge
was like taking care
of five dogs.
They didn't want
any more pets.

Henry's mother decided to make
posters to find a home
for the cat.
Henry helped her.

"Don't put the cat's picture
on them," said Henry's father,
"or we'll have that cat forever."

Henry and Mudge walked
around town with the posters.
They put one in
the grocery store
and one in the drugstore
and one in the record store.

They put a lot of them

on trees.

And Mudge ate one

by mistake.

The posters didn't say

anything about mashed prunes.

25

When Henry and Mudge
came home,
Henry's father and Henry's mother
were sitting on the couch
with the cat.

Henry's mother said,
"Cats are nice."
Henry's father said,
"Even shabby ones."

Mudge climbed onto the couch
to be with his new mother.
Henry climbed on next.
The happy cat purred and purred.

A Surprise

A lot of people saw the posters
and came to look
at the cat.

Some of them
were very rude.
They made fun of the cat.
Mudge watched them,
and his fur stood up.

A lot of people came to see
the cat because
they had lost their own.

But they always said,
"Ours is white."

Or,

"Ours is gray."

No one ever said,
"Ours looks like mashed prunes."
No one seemed to want
the cat.

Then one day
there was a surprise.
A police car parked
in front of Henry's house,
and a policeman rang
Henry's bell.

Henry and Henry's father
and Henry's big dog Mudge
went to the door.
"Can I help you?"
Henry's father asked the policeman.
(Henry's father was wondering if
Mudge had eaten somebody's purse.)

But the policeman had seen one
of the posters.
He was looking for his cat.

He said it was different
from other cats.
He said it was "unique."
He said it looked something
like mashed prunes.

Henry ran to get
the cat.
When he came back with it,
the policeman cried, "Dave!"
Henry and Henry's father
looked at each other.
"Dave?" said Henry's father.

Dave jumped out of Henry's arms
and into the policeman's arms.
The policeman kissed Dave
on the nose.
"I'm so happy to have him
back," the policeman said.

Henry looked at Mudge,
who was looking at Dave.
"Your cat likes our dog,"
Henry told the policeman.

The policeman looked at Mudge.
"I can see that," he said.
"Your dog has very clean ears."
Suddenly Henry got a
lump in his throat.
He didn't want Mudge
to lose his mother.
Even if Mudge's mother
was named Dave.

The policeman said good-bye,
and he took
his happy cat home.
When Dave the cat was gone,
Henry and Mudge felt very sad.

The towel closet was shut.

The bathtub was empty.

The dog toys were still.

Henry had to cry a little
and take a nap.
Mudge had to eat a lot of crackers
and take a nap.

Henry's father and Henry's mother
had to give them both extra hugs.

The next day
a big box was on their porch.
The note on it said:

TO MUDGE FROM DAVE.

Inside the box
were thirty giant dog bones!
And under those
was a gold police badge!

Mudge kept the dog bones
for himself.
But he shared the police badge
with Henry.
Dave the cat had taught him
very good manners.